D0827464
PARDALITA

PARDALITA

JOANA ESTRELA

Translated by
Lyn Miller-Lachmann

LQ
LEVINE QUERIDO
Montclair | Amsterdam | Hoboken

This is an Em Querido book
Published by Levine Querido

LQ
LEVINE QUERIDO

www.levinequerido.com • info@levinequerido.com
Levine Querido is distributed by Chronicle Books, LLC

Originally published in Portugal by Planeta Tangerina

Library of Congress Control Number: 2022945157
Paperback ISBN – 978-1-64614-256-9
Printed and bound in China

Published April 2023
First printing

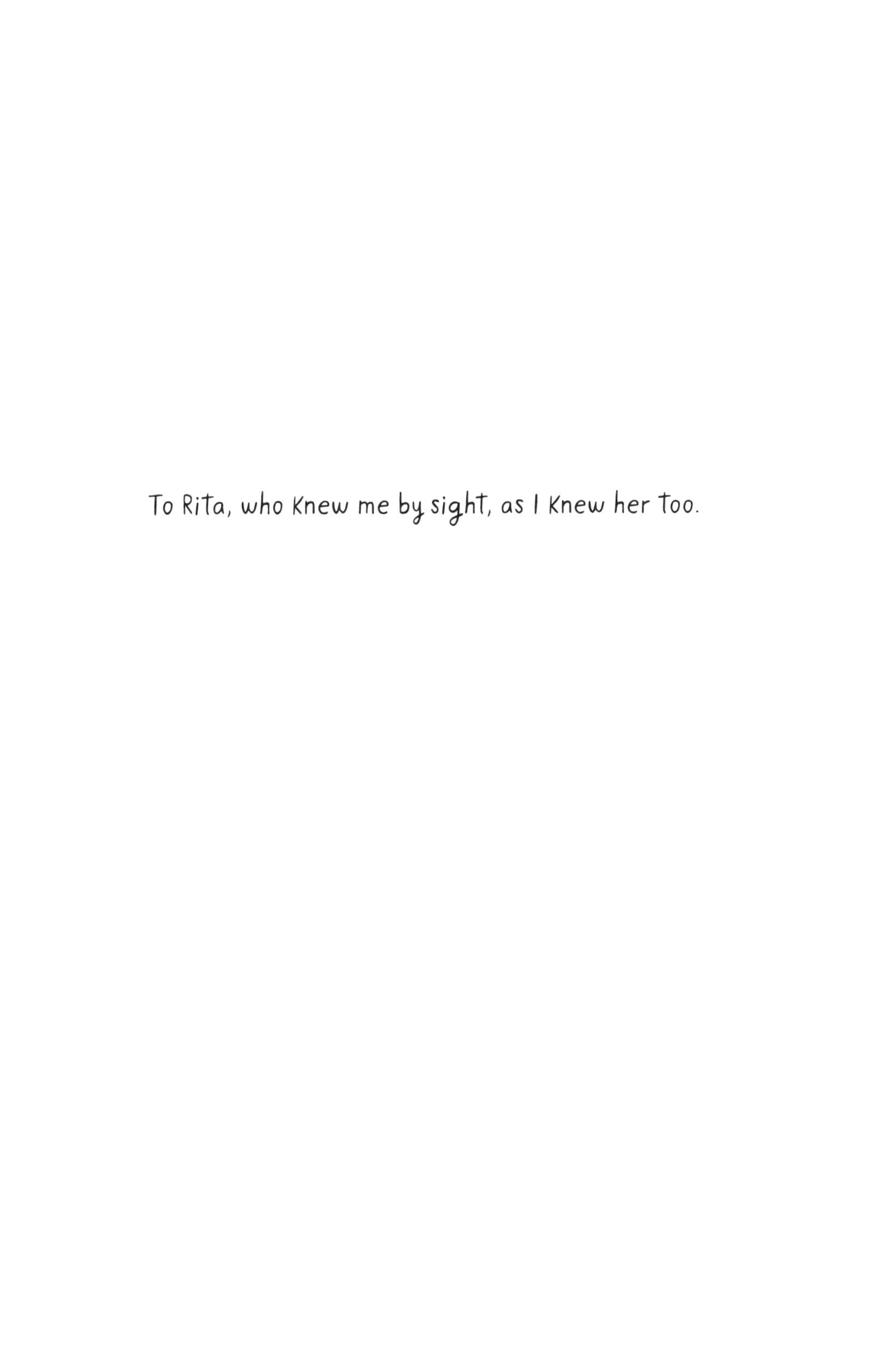

To Rita, who knew me by sight, as I knew her too.

Pardalita,

I wrote your name on the table,
without noticing. I was distracted,
and my hand formed the letters.
But maybe it wasn't really your name.
I could have meant the name of
any random person, any
random bird, an ordinary
sparrow. 
I only know it was you because this is a small town, and
everyone is up in each other's business.
For instance: the South Wing hall monitor knows my dad
is getting married again. For instance: I now know telling
the South Wing hall monitor,
"How about minding your own business, you piece of shit?"
will get a student suspended.
There are things I'm still finding out.
I was sitting by the Guidance Office door, waiting for my
mom to pick me up, and you passed (flew past).
Someone behind you called out, "Pardalita, you forgot
the paper roll!" and you spun around.
"Your head is in the clouds,"—something I would have said
if I knew you—"take the paper there. Don't forget."

I stayed home from school for two days. It wasn't bad. My mom and Zé left in the morning and I had the whole house to myself. That never happens. I didn't do anything different except turn up the music.

First English class after returning to school:

While I was out, they reviewed irregular verbs.
They're verbs that don't follow the pattern for past tense.
The teacher gave me a table with all of them and explained:
"You're not supposed to understand them. You just have to learn them by heart."
She must have noticed my annoyance because she added:
"Actually, you're in luck. English doesn't have many irregular verbs. Portuguese is much worse."
I doubt I would learn Portuguese unless I was already Portuguese. There's no reason to do it.
The only useful word in Portuguese is "obrigadinha."
You can't translate that.

Luísa and I cut each other's hair:

Three fingers,
Cut, Cut, Cut
(irregular verb).
The trick is not to wet it first.
Mine is a short bob, the way I like it.
My dad says I look like a Beatle.
Yeah Yeah Yeah

My dad:

Every other weekend I'm with my dad.
When I was a little kid, this annoyed him, because he wanted to go out and I wrecked his plans—because I had to be in bed by ten thirty, I had nightmares, I made him bring me a glass of water, or sit on the bed next to me. Sometimes, he brought me to dinner at his friends' houses and put me to bed in some random room. When it was time to leave, he would pick me up and carry my dead weight to the car. I was already too old for him to carry me around, but this was the one exception, and I took full advantage—like if I awakened, I'd still pretend to be asleep. And I forgave him for leaving me in a stranger's room.
Forgive Forgave Forgiven

THE PROBLEM WITH SHORT HAIR
IS THAT IT GROWS OUT SUPERFAST.

IT LOOKS GREAT FOR 2 WEEKS
AND THEN FALLS INTO MY EYES.

Boo, commercials.

She's like a rainbow...

Shhh! Shut up!
We weren't saying anything . . .

Whose music is this?

I think it's the Rolling Stones.
I used to listen to this.

I never see my mom getting into music. Even when she turns on the radio, she chooses talk stations.

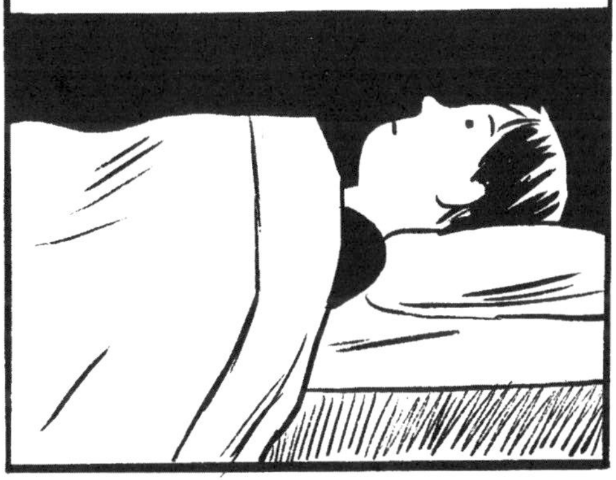
I showed her how to search for the Rolling Stones on YouTube. At night, I could hear the singer's voice from my room, on a loop.

My mom, alone in bed, listening to the same song, over and over.

My mom, thirty years ago.

My mom not as a mother.
Just a daughter. Listening to rock.
I can't even imagine!

My parents met because a friend of my dad's fell in love with a friend of my mom's.

Then they went on a bunch of dates.

At the end of the night, he walked her home.

One day when he arrived, she put him on the spot. "If you like me, you have to tell me."

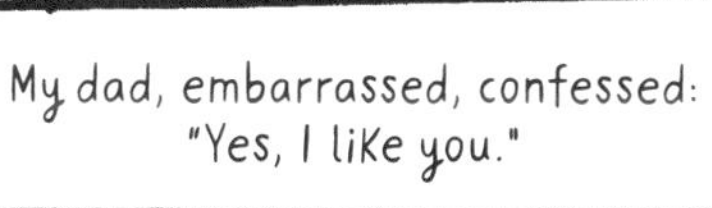
My dad, embarrassed, confessed: "Yes, I like you."

I can imagine that...my pushy mom extracting a confession.

I've lived here as long as I can remember.
I could cross the town with my eyes closed.

Yes?
It's Raquel.

Do I Know you?

LUÍSA! open up!
Hah! We already gave you money!

Luísa

I don't remember the moment Luísa and I became friends. From age four on, we were in the same class. In preschool, she married a boy named Gaspar who attended our school that year. Every time he'd pass by, I'd whisper, "Look, Luísa, your little husband," and she'd punch me hard on the arm.
In elementary school, I called her every day after school and we'd talk for hours. My mom would always say, "I don't know how you have so much to say to each other after spending the entire day together." But we did. We still do.
Speak Spoke Spoken

Luísa's parents also divorced.

Once she told me a big argument happened

because one of them seasoned the tomato salad with fine salt . . .

. . . rather than coarse salt.

I couldn't get this story out of my mind.

I think of it whenever I season salad.

and scatter it in
circles

like a ritual.

Pardalita,
Today at school I saw you
heading toward me
as I was leaving the computer lab.
I panicked and turned around.

I feel weird whenever I see you.
Maybe I envy you.

At this point, the story of my suspension has spread throughout the school and gained extra characters, action, and drama.

People generally turn away when I catch them looking at me.

In the midst of all this, I keep thinking about what it means
to know someone by sight.

We went to Fred's house after school. We heated bread rolls with ham and cheese in the microwave and watched *Titanic*.

Teenagers aren't responsible! Look at you!
I could take care of a shipwrecked child!
We've already seen this film 100 times and Fred and Luísa always manage to argue about something in the middle of it.
Last time it was about having enough space for both of them on the raft.

But they always stop talking at the end of the film.

I'm not sure about the final scene.

If she dies.

Or if it's a dream.

If every night she dreams she's back on the ship . . .

. . . with him.

At 7, Miguel stops by to pick me up and we walk back to my place together. Miguel has been my boyfriend for the past 6 months. Fred and Luísa call him The Dancer to make fun of him. He doesn't know, but I also don't think he'd care. Of all the people I know, he cares the least about what other people think of him.

At the end of *Titanic*, do you think Rose died, or is she dreaming?
Oh . . . I never saw the film.

I only Know the one part . . .

I'M THE KING OF THE WORLD!!
shhh

I haven't slept well for a week

I should say, I never sleep well. But now it's worse.
Wake Woke Woken. I toss and turn and wonder what's first:
I fall asleep, or the sun rises.
Years ago, I read a book about insomnia that suggested I pretend to fall asleep. According to the author, when we imagine the possibility of sleeping, often we manage to sleep for real.
I tried that out. I quieted and took deep breaths. I enjoyed imagining that someone came in and found me asleep.
I dedicated myself to my performance during my hours awake, thinking of how to make my false slumber more convincing. I began to try out other people's sleeping positions, my head against the pillow, my mouth half open.
In a way, it was envy: those who have trouble sleeping are in awe of those who can fall asleep anywhere.
In time, I became very good at faking sleep, and this developed into increasingly theatrical ways of changing positions, snoring, and even murmuring incoherent words or pretending I was having a nightmare.
My bed was a stage without an audience.
None of this helped. But I told myself that one day someone would write a play about a person pretending to sleep, and I'd be the best actor for the role.
Sleep Slept Slept

A few weeks ago, my mom could barely search the internet.
0

Now she runs a wildlife protection group on Facebook.
10

She uploads animal photos for adoption.
27

She has more friends online than I do!
32

45

Here's a cat.
70

Today we got our chemistry tests back and Luísa failed.
I hate this teacher with all my might. All the work I did.

What work? You didn't do any work. 0. 0. No might.

I'll show you!
Chill, you don't want to get hurt.

Ahahahah!

Cheater! Tickles don't count!

Girl fight! Sexy!
May I join?

DREAM ON!

Pfft.
Fools.

Should we go to class?

With my luck, I'm going to flunk English too.

Me at age 7

When I started elementary school I spoke so softly that no one heard me. "As red as a tomato," was how my classmates later described my face when the teacher told me to speak louder. She'd asked me the source of the Mondego River and the mouth of the Guadiana River. Rivers that I've never seen in real life and only know exist because of a map hanging on the classroom wall.
At my grandparents' house, there was a photo of my mother with her pants rolled up to her knees and her feet in the Guadiana River. And another one with her kicking a soccer ball, her shirtsleeves rolled up. My mom is like a bulldozer, rolling up everything in her way. No one can stop her. I bet in elementary school she was the first one to raise her hand. The first one to climb the wall and fall off and have to get stitches.
The first one to kiss a boy.
In the morning at the entrance to my school, which used to be her school, she would remind me to shed my shyness like an overcoat and speak louder. Then, she'd wait for me to go inside.

Things my mom wrote on the internet:

"Good morning."
"Portugal has experienced some of the world's largest destruction of ecosystems."
"With my father. In the 80s."
"Bravo!"
"No more fascism!"
"I agree!"
"Urgent!"
"Força Brasil!"
"When 26 corporations
control half of the world's wealth
something is very wrong."
"Who will take responsibility?"
"Shame."
"A winner."
"What a beautiful memory!"
"Heartbreaking."
"Today is Siblings' Day!"
"Happy Sunday!"
"When animals disappear from the face
of the Earth, how will it be?"
"Nothing to add."
"This is important."
"Says who?"
"It's time!"
"Finally, a real summer day!"
"We were here two years ago!"
"And the struggle continues."
"This is so good!"
"Good night."

Pardalita,
Today I saw you at school with
a purple skirt, green sweater,
pink beanie, red sneakers,
and yellow backpack.
She's like a rainbow.

Monstera

I noticed something different when my dad started keeping plants in his apartment. It was two years ago, more or less.

The first was an Adam's Rib plant. (Fred said its official name is *Monstera deliciosa*.)

The Monstera spread gradually and took up more and more space in the living room. The new leaves emerged rolled-up and were shiny when they opened. Now, they reach the ceiling.

After the plant, a jacket appeared. A pair of slippers. A different brand of milk in the fridge. A book that she left behind. I only met her later.

I slept over at Luísa's house.
She was grounded for a week because she failed the test.
She couldn't go out, but I could visit her.
It's good that you're here.
My mother yells at me less.

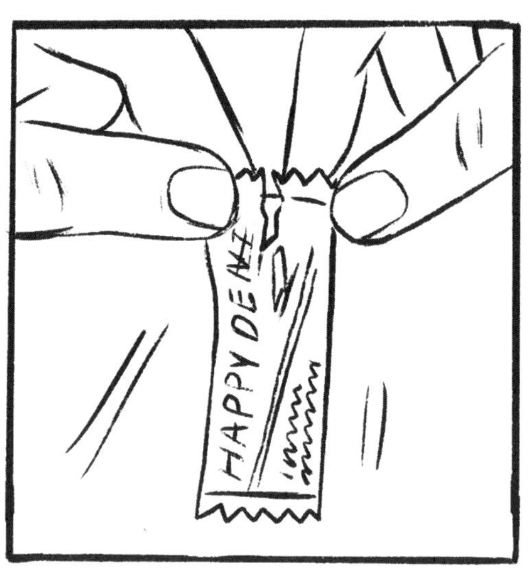
HAPPY DE

Pardalita,

I haven't seen you in 6 days.

Where have you flown?

Here and there

Sometimes when I'm with Miguel, I see myself from afar. I'm not me, but the person who passes us on the street, and sees us walking hand in hand. I'm the waiter who serves our coffee. I'm the woman sitting in front of us on the bus, the cat on the corner that we pet.
I'm a passing car, a brick wall, the trees.
Sometimes, I'm even Miguel himself. I'm the odor of his clothes when he comes from practice. I'm the hand that feels the curve of my back, the fingers that run through my hair, the lips that touch my neck.
I'm always wondering how others see us, searching for a sign that all is well. Everything so carefully rehearsed that it appears natural.
Like someone pretending to sleep.

VILA REAL
Santuário
Piscina
A4 Porto
Zona Desport
Estação

Today Luísa brought a skimpy dress in her backpack so her mother wouldn't see it.

We have ten minutes before class and Fred is helping us with math.
2 x ( )
This isn't so hard!
Not for you! We all can't be geniuses.
I'm not a genius. I just pay attention in class.

Pardalita,
you landed here.

AUDITIO
THEATER TROU

Hurry up! I still want to get something to eat.

Fred was also interested.
Not in you, but in the poster.

Fine. I think I'll go.
I know your plan.

YOU'RE DOING THEATER TO GET GIRLS!

I already know girls! What are you?
I'm a dolphin!
I'm a squid!
HEE HEE!
HA HA HA!
YOU TWO ARE HYENAS!

Me at age 6

One day a teacher asked Luísa to read a number from the blackboard, and she said she didn't know. The teacher moved the pointer to another number and said, "What number is this?" Luísa didn't know. She continued to point to more numbers, to all the numbers, and Luísa kept saying she didn't know. She couldn't read the words on the board either.

Seated next to Luísa, I was shocked and confused because it wasn't true. She knew all her numbers, but why was she lying about it?

Several weeks later I arrived to class late. The other kids were already there, running around the multipurpose room. Luísa was sitting on the floor outside, crying behind a new pair of glasses, round with green frames.

She wore a green sweater the same shade as the glasses, the kind of style that I always adored. When she showed up, the kids had teased her, and she'd refused to go inside.

"But they look good on you!" I lied. She blew her nose in her handkerchief and I took her hand and knocked on the door for us to enter.

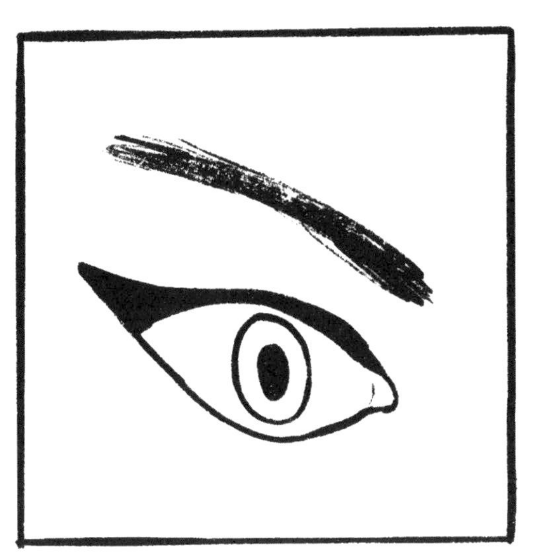

Wow! I can't believe you can do that.

How do you manage to touch your eye?

It's easy! Want me to touch yours?
Uh, no thanks.

Luísa's cousin is a psychic, and Luísa has been talking nonstop about her for weeks. Her office is on the bottom floor of the Tem-Tem mall. The sign on the door said, "Holistic Wellness Center," but everyone knows she tells fortunes.

We were worried that someone would see us there, but the mall was nearly vacant and the only shops that remained were real estate and other offices.
LUIS S LOPES
Advogado

She described Luísa's future and read her Tarot with playing cards.

Afterward she offered me a palm reading.

There's someone new in your life.

I have a new boyfriend, Miguel.

That's not it. I see a name starting with P.

I don't know who it is.

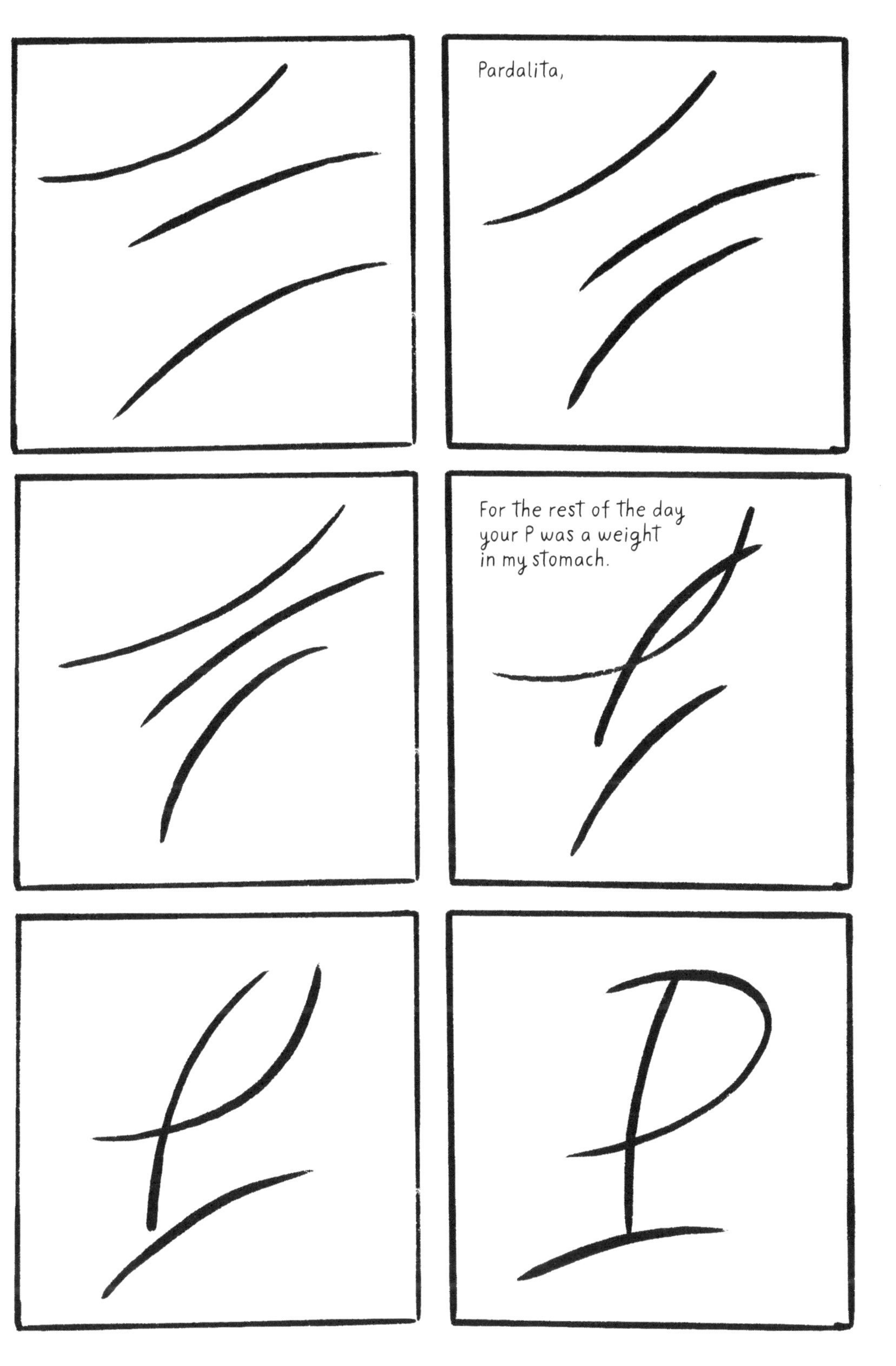
Pardalita,
For the rest of the day your P was a weight in my stomach.

Yuck, what is this?
It's . . . pink.

They're beet meatballs.
I found the recipe on the internet.

And there's salad? How trendy!
Don't exaggerate . . .

. . . I always make salad.

But usually it's just lettuce.

So yesterday your cousin Ana Teresa forwarded some ridiculous articles . . .

Saying that London is no longer an English city, that it's full of foreigners.

I reminded her that she lives there and is definitely not English either. She needs more self-respect.

That didn't go well.
Are we surprised?

She said she's European. It's different.

I don't think she's going to invite us for New Year's this year.

I hope you two don't mind. For me, it's a relief.

5 messages from Miguel

I'll answer tomorrow, I have no brain today.
Better yet, I have no stomach.
Better yet, I have no appendix.
(The last one is true.)

Becoming a writer

We have a new student teacher in Portuguese class. She's nice. She was talking with me about my essay and said that I should become a writer. I laughed. I thought of telling her that at this moment I'm writing only one letter: P. Maybe later my interest will expand to the rest of the alphabet.

CHOOSE CHOSE CHOSEN

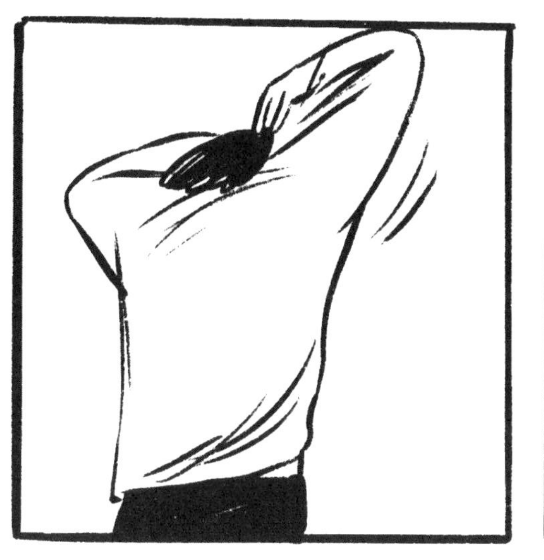

Nothing fits

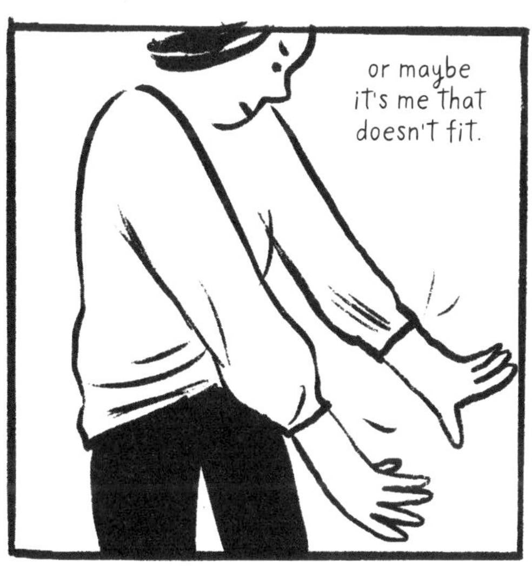
or maybe it's me that doesn't fit.

Break

I didn't feel like seeing Miguel so I hid in the library during lunch break. I was the only one there, except for a small but noisy group of teachers enjoying a cake in the shape of pi.
The student teacher from my Portuguese class was also there, assigned the interminable (literally)
task of hanging posters on the wall with the number
3.141592653589793238462643383279502884197169
39937510582097494459230781640628620899862803
48253421170679821480865132823066470938446095
5058223172535940812848111745028410270193852 . . .
She stopped when she passed me.
"I'm sorry that we're distracting you from studying."
"It's okay. I was just reading."
I don't know why I did this, but I held up the *Anthology of Classic Greek Poetry* to show her I wasn't reading easy books.

How nice! Which poet are you up to?
Alcman.
Sophia de Mello Breyner wrote a poem that's called "Adapted from Alcman."
9 3 2 3
It goes:
The muse, the siren
Her song loud and pure.
Is that all?
It's all you need.

You think he's boning the student teacher?
What?! No!

I bet he tried everything. He met her after class and said, "Would you like to feel my Portuguese tongue?"
Shut up! That's disgusting!

He went out with a student. Remember Tânia Big Boobs? They had an affair.
LUÍSA!

Oh, that's just what they called her. It wasn't her real last name. She had top grades in Portuguese and failing everywhere else.
That doesn't mean anything.
I'm flunking too. I should seduce one of these teachers so I can raise my grades to average.
Oh! Oh! He's coming back. Here's your chance!

High school is a fishbowl.

Me at age 5

I remember sitting in the backseat of the car and my parents (they were still together) spent the entire trip talking about people I didn't know. What they bought, their new job, who got married, who said what about who.
Our car was a beat-up old Renault 4. The back seat didn't have seatbelts and the side windows only opened a few inches. Moss grew in the rubber seal around the glass.
Later, when they separated, my father sold the car. Or was it before?

Tell Told Told

My mom used to say: "Secrets don't tell themselves. That's why they're called secrets. When people complain that secrets get out, they have only themselves to blame. Shouldn't have told anyone in the first place."
I don't think my mom is a person with many secrets.

It's Sunday

No one's home again. I don't know where they went.
I fixed myself lunch: omelet on bread.
On television, the news crawl read, "Portugal recorded its highest number of foreigners." Above the text, seated between two men in suits, the woman host asked, "Are we prepared to receive more immigrants?"
What immigrants? I never met any.

I wanted to message Fred and Luísa to watch this, but my phone screen was full of alerts reminding me of the messages I still haven't opened.

Miguel broke up with me.
I expected it. I was being a jerk to him.
Hurt Hurt Hurt

I switched to airplane mode
but it feels like I've landed.

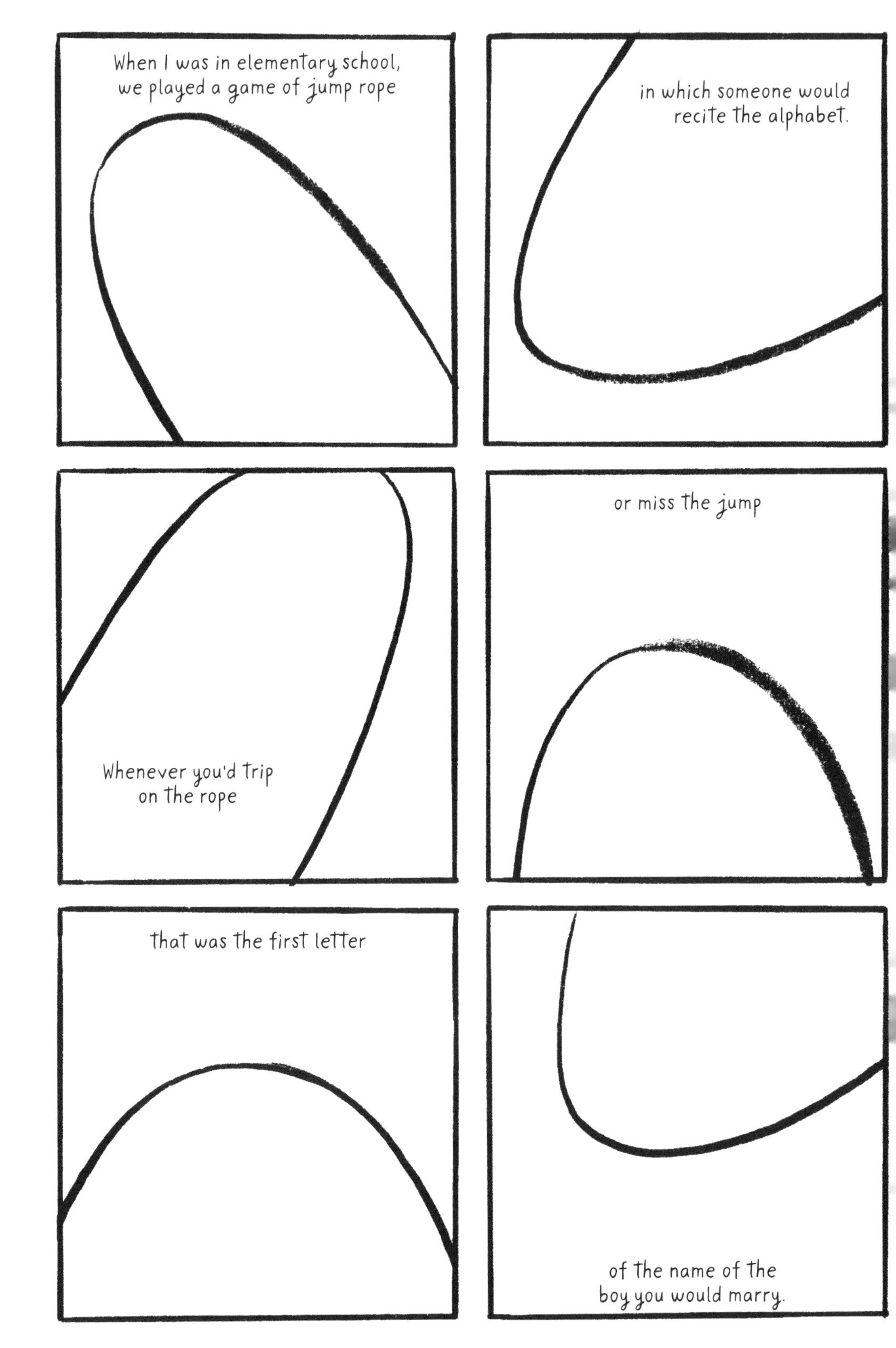
When I was in elementary school,
we played a game of jump rope
in which someone would
recite the alphabet.
Whenever you'd trip
on the rope
or miss the jump
that was the first letter
of the name of the
boy you would marry.

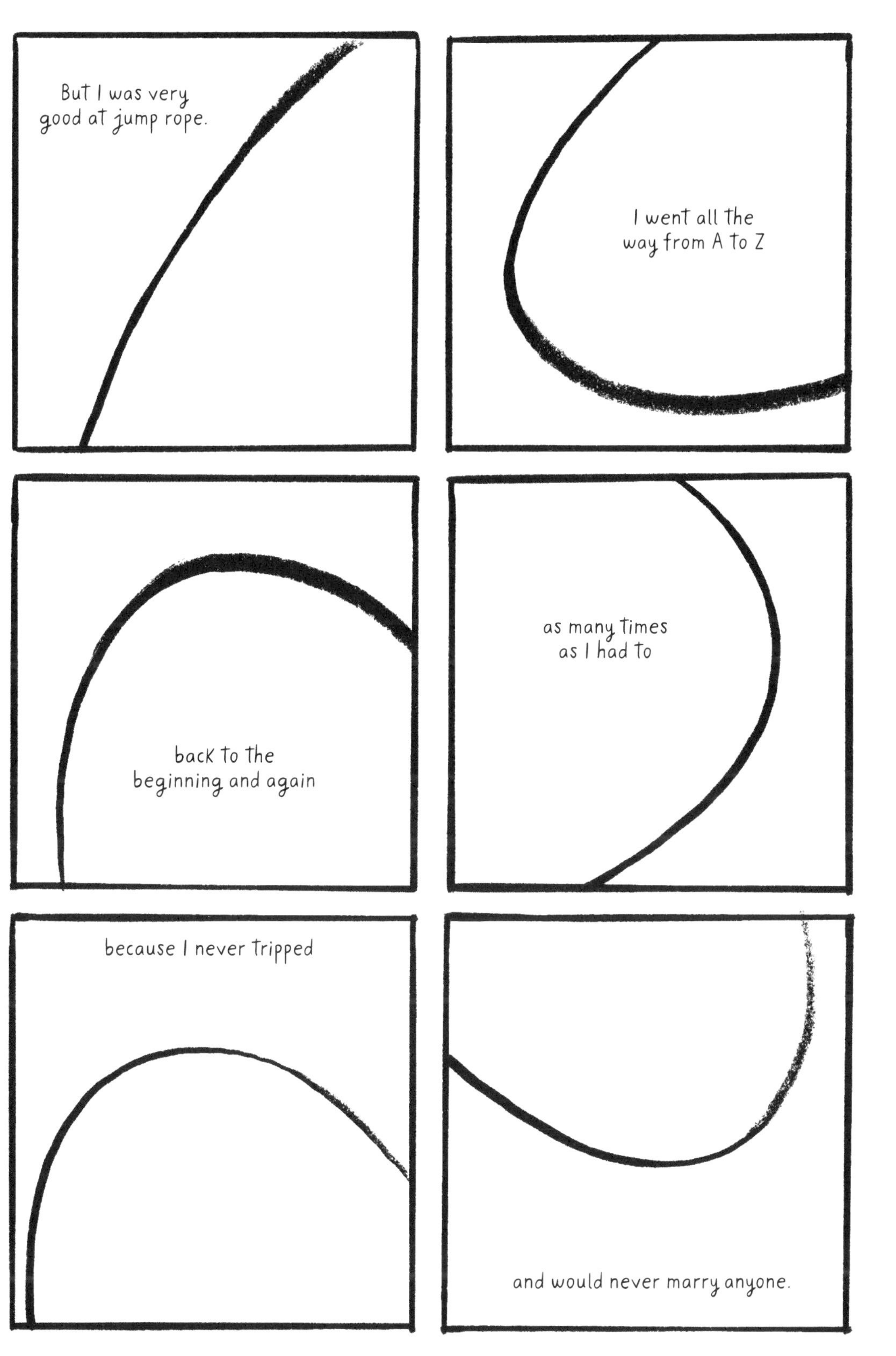
But I was very good at jump rope.
I went all the way from A to Z
back to the beginning and again
as many times as I had to
because I never tripped
and would never marry anyone.

Not my day

I can barely drag my pen across the notebook page.
The ruled lines look like grids
and my biology textbook is staring at me
dumbstruck, waiting to be learned by heart.

And what if?

There are more people who are, of course.
There are celebrities who are.
There's that actress. In America.
I saw on a magazine cover where
she said she was.
One letter from a group of letters.
But maybe I'm not even.
How does a person know they are?
Is there a test?
Wait. I remember now.
That poet who lived 2500 years ago
on an island in Greece.
There were people 2500 years ago who were.
The problem is
I'm not seeing anyone else
who may be
in this place
in this moment.
Someone who isn't
an actress in America
or an ancient poet.
Because I can't be the only one
who is
here
now.
And what if?

Miguel stopped by to return some things I'd left at his house.

I had nothing to give him in return.

Here it is.

Thanks.

I miss you.
Me too.

It's weird that we don't talk now.
You're right.

In the bag were:
A math workbook, guitar picks, a pen advertising cough syrup, 3 CDs, and the flyer from a concert that we saw together. The flyer was trash but he kept it anyway.

Fred made me promise to go with him to audition for the theater troupe, to give him moral support.

The theater troupe is located in the Community and Cultural Center next to the church, one of those places you can pass by every day and not know it's there. When we arrived, the door was open to the inside, and Pardalita leaned against it to welcome everyone and check off names on a paper.

She found "Frederico" on the list, then looked at me. I must have said something about being there just to watch, I don't know, because she took my arm and invited me inside. "Don't you want to audition too? Come! Try out!"

I'm not sure what scared me the most: the idea of auditioning, or her hand that tugged me. As I seriously considered the possibility of leaving my arm there, and running away, Fred gave me an expression of don't-leave-me-here-alone-for-God's-sake, and Pardalita said, "There are other things you can do besides acting. You can help with lights or sound or scenery. I'll put your name down here, OK? It's Raquel, right?"

I didn't trust myself to say anything, so I just nodded.

They called us one at a time.
When it was my turn, I went into a rehearsal room.
Inside was a space heater, a three-way extension cord, a coat rack, and a table where Boy 1, Boy 2, and Pardalita were sitting.
They asked my name. (Raquel.)
How old I was. (16)
If I'd ever done theater before. (No.)
If I knew how to do anything. (What?)
Something theater-related. (I can play guitar.)
What poem I wanted to read. (Poem?)

We asked people to bring a poem to recite.
Do you know anything by heart?

I think I know one.

The muse
The siren

Her song loud and pure

That's it.

Very succinct, thank you!
I don't think you'd seen anything that quick.
Pardalita, you're so pretty.
There, it's said. Say Said Said.

In the end, we both joined.
Fred as an actor
and me doing sound.
PEIXARIA

This is going to be awkward.

When I got home, my mother was lying on the sofa with the computer on her stomach, which made her look a bit childish. She typed rapidly, comments for some kind of discussion, muttering under her breath from time to time. She's been volunteering at the animal shelter on Tuesday and Thursday afternoons and on Sunday cleaning the beach.
She's always rushing around.
She's getting a good tan.
When I arrived, she made me take the clothes out of the washing machine.
"I think we should stop washing our clothes altogether because of the environment and saving water and everything."
She smiled while staring at the monitor.
"Don't give me any ideas."

You're saying I'm the only one who's not in theater?
Yeah, you, the most dramatic of all!

HOW DARE YOU!

THE HORROR!

MY POOR HEART

gaaaaaaaah!

Fine, I'm getting food. Want anything?
Bring me a creampuff.

Just inside the Community and Cultural
Center is a living room.
The furniture is secondhand and all
the chairs are different.
The combination is odd but inviting.

So is the group.

Day one

Pardalita gave us a guided tour. Fred and I (shy and quiet now that we didn't have Luísa to break the ice) followed her through a maze of hallways, full of cardboard boxes with handwritten labels like "rice hats", "angel wings", "fly suits" . . .
There was a broken table and sofas piled up in a corner. If it weren't for the thick layer of dust on everything, I would have thought they were moving.
I stepped carefully to avoid tripping over the tangle of cables on the floor. Sheets covered some piles of stuff, with a sign that read "DON'T TOUCH".
Pardalita showed us what was behind the doors, with one exception:
"We now lock up the costumes and props because we were robbed."

For now, the plan was for me to take
part in the warm-ups.
"So we're all on the same page."

Pardalita,
I tried to sit as far away
from you as possible.
But since we were in a
circle, the farthest away
meant facing you directly.
Not the best plan.

Standing

The director said, "Eyes closed, feet apart."
She asked us to shift our body weight. First toward the left foot, then the right, then heels, then toes. Leaning until the moment we thought we'd fall.
The room smelled of sweat and wood. I peeked a little to make sure the other fifteen people were still in the circle, swaying, and I wasn't the only one.
"Now decide where your weight goes. As if a breeze were shaking you."
I only heard the faint sounds of the floor creaking and cars far away.
Finally, she asked us to find our center and transfer our weight toward it. "Don't open your eyes. You don't need to see. Feeling is enough."
I searched in darkness, but every time I thought I found my center, it moved away. Have I always been this scattered?

TODAY: MY HAIR IS PERFECT.

Dinner

Mom made a lentil curry and announced that as of today she's a vegetarian.
I think this is very unfair, because she's the only person in the house who knows how to cook. Couldn't she wait two more years until I left for university?
Bye bye meat
Eat Ate Eaten

A tour

I take out my student ID to pay for a grilled sandwich at the snack bar and stare at it while I wait. The passport-style photo is tiny; one can barely make out who I am. It has my name, student number, and in the background a large photo of the school. I think it's funny that my place on the ID card is so insignificant compared to the school. In fact, the photo is only of the A wing. Half of it is hidden by pine trees at the entrance. Every now and then, a stray cat gets stuck up there and security has to call the fire department. I used to think those things only happened in movies and cartoons, but here I found out it's real.

Around the B wing, the trees are shorter. Some of them have berries and kids compete to see who can collect the most. They say the berries are alcoholic.

If we go all the way down, we get to the Physical Education wing and next to it the outdoor courts and fields. The ground has colored lines for various team sports and is full of acorns from the oak tree planted next to the benches. When I pass by and find a perfect acorn (whole, shiny, with an intact cupule), I stick it in my pocket. I don't do anything with them, they just sit in my jacket from one year to the next, until I dump them in the trash to make room for new perfect acorns.

There's a chain link fence that encloses the playing fields and bushes on the other side. I don't know if they're part of the school, but they're impassible. Behind the oak tree is the way to the snack bar, the cafeteria, and the student lounge. Here the trees are young and skinny, tied to stakes for support. The sun shines hot and kids play ping-pong on cement tables.

Continuing to the right is the main gate, which faces the pine trees, the stray cats, and the A wing where we started.

When we don't have classes, we walk in circles around the campus, which is what all caged animals do. Normally we talk, but today the three of us were silent, hearing only the sound of our footsteps on gravel. Luísa broke the stillness.

"Who is that?"

Among the cedars in the distance, Pardalita was dashing to class late and waving hello.

In theater
we run
jump
sweat
twist
stretch
turn
stop
bend
dance
shiver
shake
warm up
pace
spin

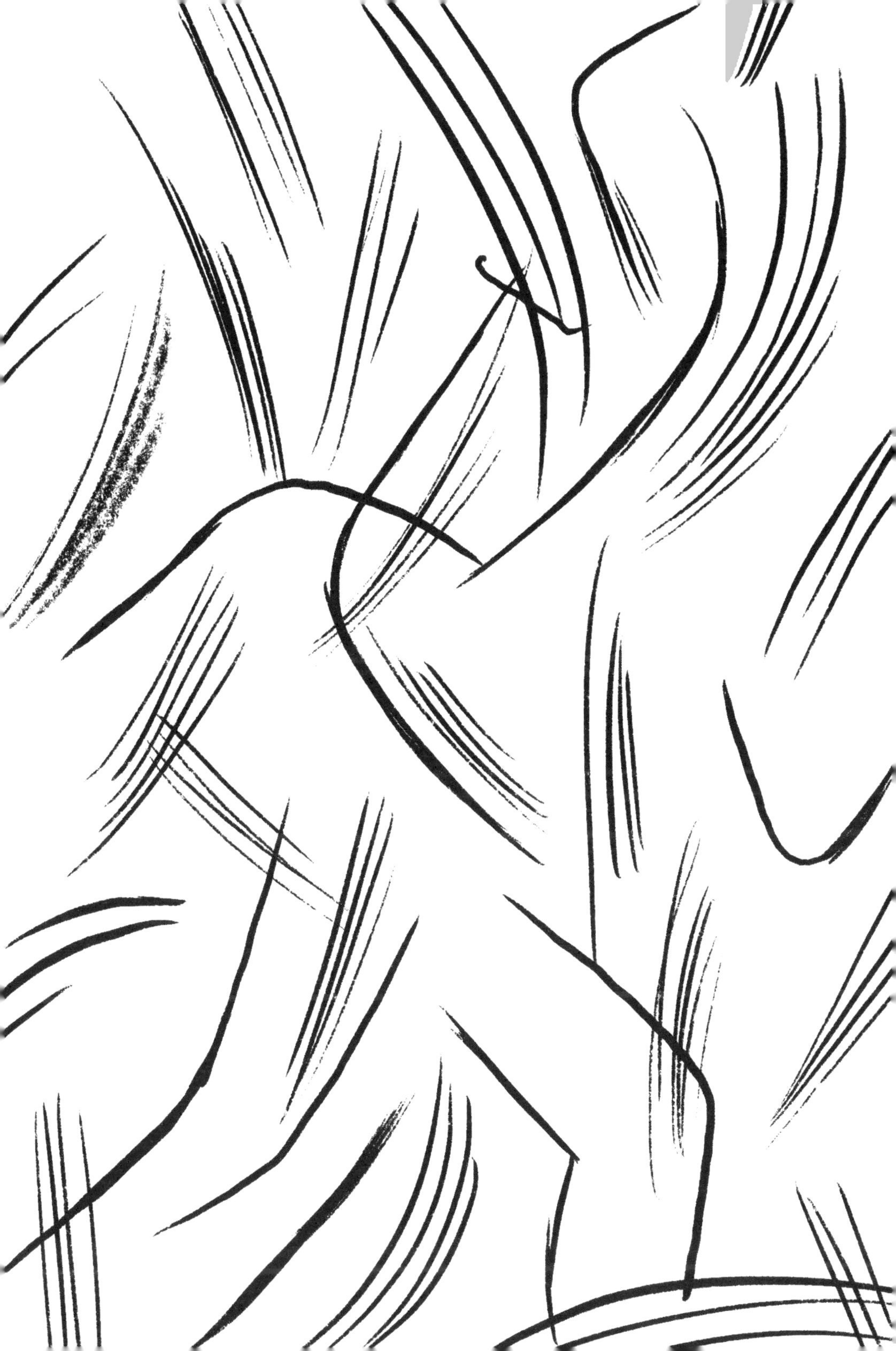

Finally, we all lie down.

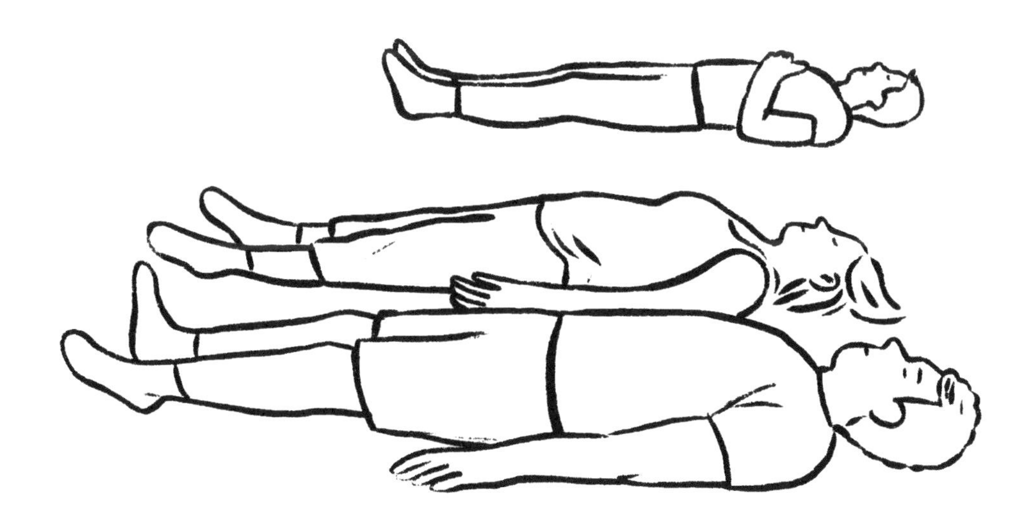

Breathe in through your nose, breathe out through your mouth. Fill your lungs. Feel the rhythm.
aa...
Louder.
aaa...
The sound wants out.
Like a sigh at the end of a long journey.
aaaa...
Like a thirsty traveler drinking a cup of water.
aaaaa...
Let it transform into sound.
aaaaaa...

It's not suffering, but the opposite.
aaaa
Relief.
aaa
aaa
aaa
aa
aaa
aa
a!
aaa
aa
a!

Then she asked us to hold the sound for as long as possible.

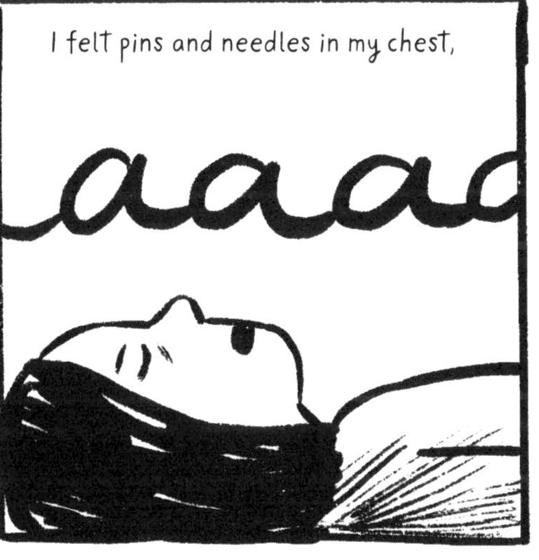
I felt pins and needles in my chest,

a vibration that came from me

and from everyone around me.

After the session we hung out by the door to the center. Something was different. Not just us being flushed and sweaty. We kept talking, trying to hold back the day's end. When someone had to leave, we hugged them as if we'd always done this, as if we'd been friends forever.

When I finally left, it was almost midnight. Walking home, I saw a group of workmen painting the roadway. Yellow crosswalks, my favorites.

Italy

My mom was driving me to school and I was staring out the window. The municipal pools appeared and disappeared, the trees slipped past us, we passed the Pizzeria Ricardo, then the fairgrounds, the church, the World War I monument . . .

I tried to imagine seeing my town for the first time, but it was almost impossible.

On the radio, more of what I knew by heart:

The weather, the traffic, the news, minus an hour in the Azores. It was so familiar, one thing after the other, and I barely noticed my mom blinking and the car pulling to the side of the road.

I thought the car had broken down, but she'd stopped to listen to the radio. Something about a boat. Italy. A Portuguese guy accused of human trafficking.

As soon as the announcer moved on to the next item, Mom started yelling at him.

"Are we in the Middle Ages? When did it become illegal to save someone? A life is a life!"

I suspect that if I weren't in the car with English class at 8:30 she would have turned around and driven the Citroen all the way to Italy.

You don't talk about this at school.

Uh, I don't think so.

Doesn't it bother you?

There's nothing I can do.

Oh.

Pardalita,
Rehearsal ended and again we all stood outside.
One by one, the others left. Only their cigarette butts remained.
I stuck around because you stayed too.
I'm so pathetic, I'll end up annoying you.
If you told me to lie down in the middle of the sidewalk, with the cigarette butts, I'd do it.
I just want to hang around. I don't want to be a pest.

New message
To: Pardalita
Hi! What are you doing today?
Send Sent Sent

Nothing! Want to go for coffee?

We went for coffee

I don't talk much, but seated in a plastic chair on Café Central's terrace, I couldn't shut up. We talked about everything—future, present, and past perfect.

Things I didn't know about
Pardalita that I know now:

1. She lives above a shopping center. The building is purple and she detests the color.
2. She has nothing against purple in general. It's that purple, that building, in particular.
3. Her glasses are unbreakable. She handed them to me and said I couldn't break them. True, I couldn't, but I also didn't try very hard.
4. She folds a napkin while she speaks.
5. She smells of clean clothes.
6. After drinking her coffee, she emptied the rest of the sugar packet into her cup and stirred it with a spoon.
7. When she ties back her hair, she pats the top her head twice to make sure she's picked up every strand.
8. She wants to know if I like theater.
9. She wants to know what I like besides theater.
10. She wants to know if I'd like to share a grilled ham and cheese sandwich because she can't eat the whole thing.

Me at age 12

Once at the beach a weeverfish stung me. At first it didn't hurt that much and I didn't tell my mother because I didn't want to bother her. I thought, "Don't make waves, Raquel, it'll go away." But it didn't go away. I felt a hot throbbing up my leg, pulsing with my blood. My ears began to buzz and I became dizzy. I don't know how I stood it for so long.

I don't recall how I got to the hospital, but I do remember the girl sitting in the bed next to me. She was blond and had freckles all over. I could even see them through her black sheer stockings and was mesmerized. It never occurred to me that someone could have freckles on their legs. It was the most beautiful thing I'd seen on anyone's body.

Returning home, I noticed a sign taped to the utility poles on our street.

Inside, the same cat,
but alive and on a living
room chair.

Pardalita,
At rehearsal today they started the warm-ups with tongue twisters. I, with my twisted tongue, read them silently. The tag on your sweater was sticking out, touching your neck. I try to watch you when you're not looking, so what I saw was the tag moving from one side of the room to the other, behind your back. The tag passed, and with the passage of time, I became so attached to it that it upset me when someone fixed the tag by sticking it back inside your clothes.

Act I
Scene 1

Characters: RAQUEL, MOM, and CAT

RAQUEL is lying on the sofa reading, and CAT is in his usual chair. The TV has tomorrow's weather forecast. High of 70 and low of 59. It's nighttime.

MOM enters holding her computer.

MOM: Raquel, where do you find torrents?

RAQUEL (sits with her hand on the open page of the book): What?

MOM (more hesitant now): I need to download a film . . . and they tell me there are torrents. Like storms.

RAQUEL (stands): Ah! (She holds the computer in the crook of her arm and begins to type something while her mom looks over her shoulder.) It has nothing to do with weather. It's Torrent.

MOM: Then why do they name it that?

CAT: Meow.

It's been five days and no one's called about the cat.

So I think it's our cat now.

He doesn't seem to miss anyone.

Rather, he gives the impression that the house is his

and we're the intruders.

Does he do anything?
He's already old.

Pardalita,
This is how my day began.
Torrential rain. A real torrent, not downloads.
A girl goes out in the rain. That girl is me.
The girl decides that running will make her wetter. So she slows, looking at the ground to avoid the puddles.
The girl feels the rain is a punishment the universe has designed especially for her.
Later, there's a girl in the rain.
Not the same girl, this one is you.
The girl carries a shabby umbrella.
Its rod is bent and rusty.
It's a miracle the umbrella still works and the wind hasn't blown it apart. (When a gust broke Mom's umbrella, she called it toast, and I thought of a sweet wind sprinkling the busted umbrella with sugar and cinnamon.)
The girl with the battered umbrella goes up to the girl without an umbrella.
The two fit underneath, and they walk shoulder to shoulder.

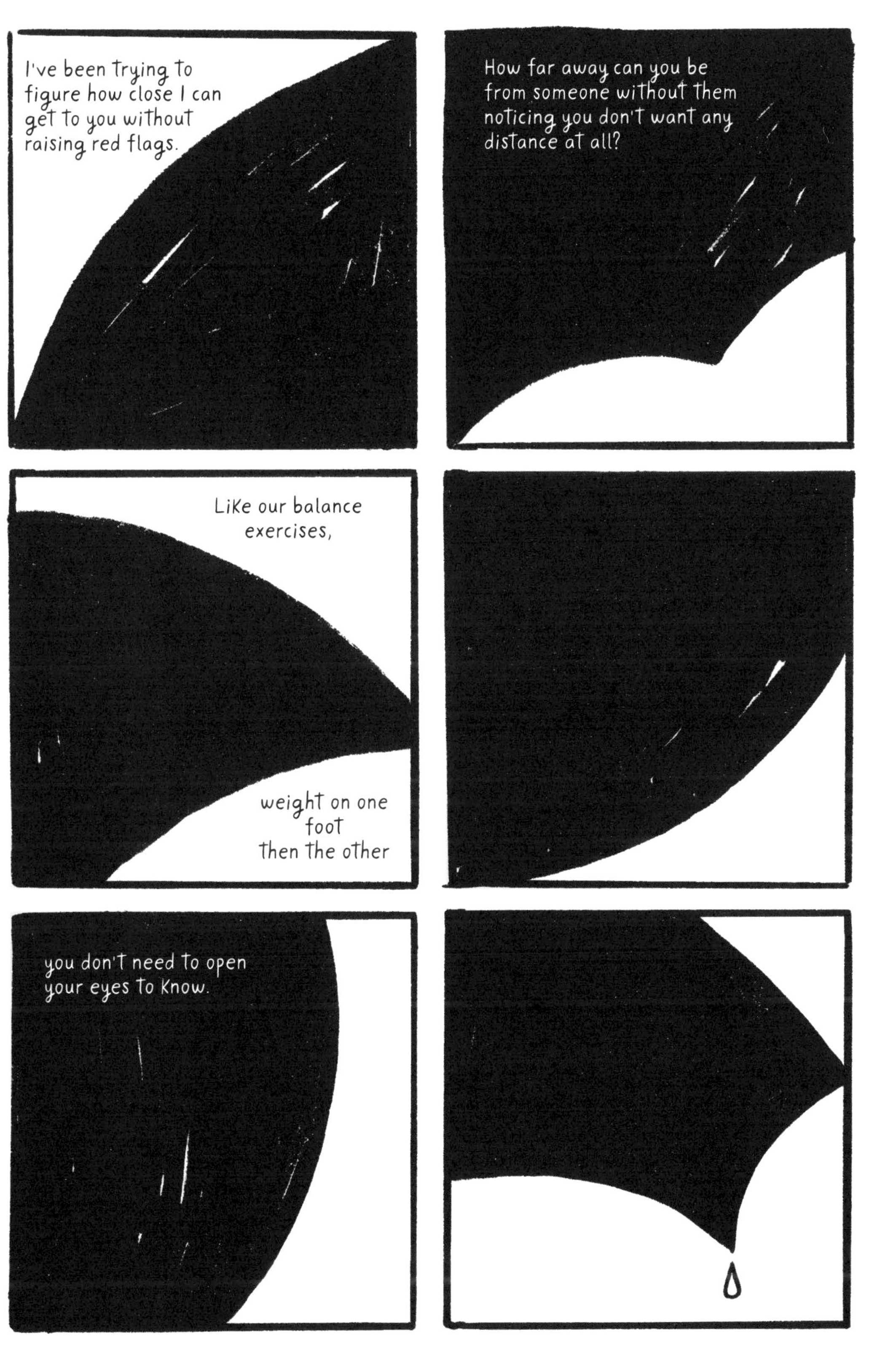

I've been trying to figure how close I can get to you without raising red flags.
How far away can you be from someone without them noticing you don't want any distance at all?
Like our balance exercises,
weight on one foot then the other
you don't need to open your eyes to know.

Me at age 13:
What are you doing?
We're seeing who's gay.

How?
Fingers. If your ring finger is longer than your index finger, it's because you are.

Carlos is a fag, poor thing.
Let me see yours.

Ooh! Yours are exactly the same size.

Haha, you're neither one or the other.

Try to measure this.

I think Luísa and Fred suspect something.
But we don't talk about it. It's a tacit agreement.
Don't ask, don't tell.
I tell them, "Today I can't, I'm going for coffee with Pardalita," or, "I have to go. I'm meeting Pardalita at the park," or even, "I'm going to the movies with Pardalita but I'll hang out with you later." They say nothing.

Raquel, is your dad bald?

No . . .

Let's see if you're telling the truth.

Is the opposite of the truth
a lie?

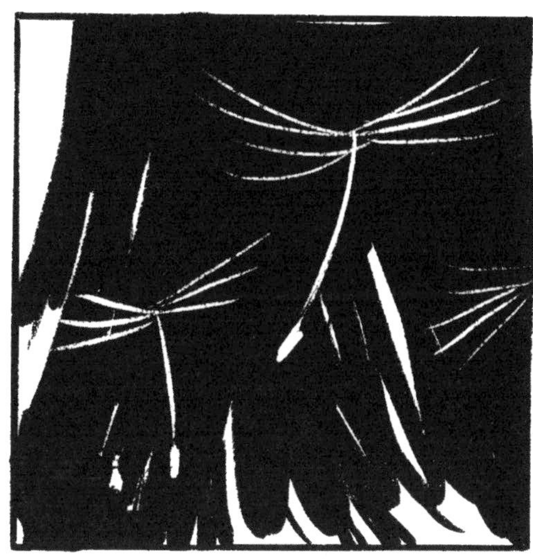

Or is there something else in the middle,

hidden between the two?

Hero and Leander

The theater troupe will begin rehearsing the play.
I don't have the script yet, but Pardalita told me:
"It's an ancient and tragic story."
"How ancient?"
"The first version appeared in one of Ovid's books. But it must have been told before."
"What's it about?"
"Hero and Leander."
"Is one of the two heroes of the story named Hero?"
"Yes, but the woman."
"The hero is a woman?"
"The woman's named Hero."
"And Leander is a man, right?"
"For sure. That much they know. It's a love story."
"Let me guess: they meet but they can't be together. They try to get together and then one dies and the other commits suicide."
"Basically, that's it. But do you want me to tell you or not?"
"Yes, please."
"Okay. Hero is a priestess of Aphrodite."
"That sounds like a euphemism. What does a priestess of Aphrodite do?"
"I don't know. Prays to Aphrodite. Like a friar. But she lives alone, in a tower overlooking the sea."

"What sea does she see from her window?"
"Good that you ask, because it's very important to the story. She sees the Hellespont Strait."
"Does that place still exist?"
"Yes, but it has another name, the Dardanelles. It's a channel that links the Aegean Sea and the Sea of Marmara. It separates Europe from Asia. In this story Leander and Hero are also separated. One lives on one bank and one lives on the other."
"How do they meet?"
"At a fair. Leander crosses the strait to enjoy the celebration and Hero is also there. He falls in love at first sight and tries to seduce her."
"How?"
"He tells her that if she wants to be a priestess of the goddess of love, she needs some experience in the matter."
"How clever."
"And he convinces her! They agree that if Hero wants company at night, all she has to do is set a candle in the tower window. And Leander will swim across the strait, guided by the light."
"Is that possible?"
"What?"
"If that place still exists, is it possible to swim across?"
"Some people have done it, I think. But you need to be a strong swimmer."
"Or you need to have a very good reason."
"Or that. One night Hero lights the candle in the window. Maybe she never expected anything to happen. Maybe she thought he was a big talker, making the kind of promises guys make. Maybe she was bored and lit the candle just to see what would happen . . .

But she didn't know that during that entire time, Leander had his eyes on the horizon, waiting. And the moment he saw the light on the opposite bank, he left and began to swim toward it. He arrived naked and dripping wet, shivering from cold."
"Why didn't he take a boat?"
"Because someone could have seen him."
"He could have disguised himself."
"You're very practical. Do you want to know what happens next?"
"Yes, please."
"She gives him her clothes to warm up."
"Does he wear women's clothes?"
"Yes. And they sleep together. In the morning, he swims back home. This goes on all summer long. When winter approaches, the sea becomes more dangerous. Leander still tries to swim across, but he's caught in a storm. In the morning, his body washes up on the coast. Hero sees it from her window and throws herself from the tower."
"How sad."

If it were you, you would have disguised yourself.
For sure.

I would have dressed up as a tuna and taken a boat.
Haha!

In this scene, are you Leander?
I suppose so.

I think I'll always be the person who crosses the river . . .

. . . dressed as a fish.
Or some other sea creature.

The cat

We now know why nobody claimed the cat. He's completely out of control. He must have been abandoned for being mean as a snake. Whenever I pass in the hallway, he hisses at me. He attacked Maria da Luz while she was cleaning, so now whenever she comes we have to put on gloves to lock him in his carrier.
But my mom adores him, and he adores her and only her.

Even when he sleeps, he grumbles. His eyelids and whiskers quiver and he groans.
How can a cat dream? I thought it was just a human thing—that a cat dreaming is like him riding a bicycle and going to school.
Does the cat dream of attacking Maria da Luz?
Or does he dream that he's a wild cat in the forest?
A kind of ancestral dream, the same for all cats, repeated every night?

Dream

Pardalita and I were in my grandmother's kitchen.
It no longer exists but was the way I remember
with the white cupboards and the floor tiles with
geometric patterns.
I was barefoot and asked, "Am I in your personal
bubble?" I don't know why I was speaking in English.
Pardalita said "No" in Portuguese.
I stepped toward her and asked, "And now?" She said no
again.
I took another step and asked anew. This went on until
I had no more room to step, until there was no distance
between us. And the answer was always no, and then I
woke up.

Rehearsal

They lowered the lights and began the first meeting scene, when Leander sees Hero and immediately falls in love. In the darkest corner of the fairground, he seizes his opportunity. The script says that Hero stared at the ground, hiding her face flushed with shame while she smoothed the dirt with her feet.
She tightened her tunic around her shoulders and said: "Foreigner, your words could move a stone. Who taught you such tricks to deceive a maiden?"

I Went to the Used Book Fair at Town Hall

I bought a tiny book that fit in my shirt pocket. The cover read: "Albano Martins The Essence of Alcaeus and Sappho Fifty Cents."
Inside read: "The portrait of Sappho that Alcaeus has bequeathed us has served to nourish the conviction that he harbored a secret (or if confessed, then rejected) love for her." What a sad parenthesis.
Alcaeus and Sappho are together in the same book because they lived on the same island at the same time. And because Alcaeus wrote about her. She may have written about him, no one knows. Together on a tiny island. Together in a tiny book. One who liked the other.

When I return home I search for images of the island. The first photo shows a beach covered with life vests and black swollen things that once were boats.

New window. Find the island on a map.
Lesbos

Zoom out.

Sunday

I woke up too early. I brought a box of cereal to bed and ate it lying down. I made a mental list of the sounds outside.

1. Garage door of the building.
2. The neighbor's dog barking at the other neighbor's dog.
3. Music from the evangelical church service (sometimes I see them from the window. It's a small congregation. At the end of the service they usually sing praise songs to someone.)
4. Kisses and goodbyes at the church entrance.
5. The cars driving off.
6. The street once again silent. I hear only sparrows.

Think Thought Thought

Leander

We came to Fred's house to help him rehearse the play. Luísa and I pushed the table aside, turned off the television, and sat on the sofa to be his audience.
In one of the final scenes, in which Leander decides to dive into the sea and risk the storm, Fred stands in the center of the rug in the center of the room. But the rug is not a rug now. It's the sand on the beach in Sestus, and his feet sink in softly while he steps backward and forward.
And Fred is not Fred. He's Leander, and he seems older and tenser. His eyes search the horizon. He sees dark clouds in the distance and says to himself:
"Why do I feel unsettled every time the water is unsettled?"
He takes off his sneakers and stuffs his socks inside. He sheds his jacket and conveys the sensation that we aren't there, or rather, that we aren't supposed to be there.
He looks again at the sea, which is where the wall between the living room and the kitchen should be.
It's hard to tell if he's sad or angry.
The scene ends when he chooses to dive into the water and walks barefoot in our direction.

I can never trust you again! You're too good an actor.
How did you learn to fake so well?
I don't know if faking is so much harder than not faking.

From the look of it,
my mother is organizing
some kind of
demonstration.

I first found out
on the internet.

During the break, I met Pardalita at the 12th grade art room. They keep the door unlocked when a student needs to finish a project. The rest of the class had already gone, but they'd left behind the distinct odor of turpentine that they used to clean the brushes.

Who made the original?
Maria Helena Vieira da Silva.

But I also have some of my own to show you.
I mean, they're all mine

but these came from my ideas.

If everything goes smoothly Pardalita will study Painting in Lisbon at the end of September.

Five months from now.

And you? Do you know what you want to do after high school?
Not really.

There's nothing you like?
There are things.

You still have time.

A friend of mine's in his first year of Painting and he's showing his work next weekend.
I'm thinking of going. Do you want to come?

I WANTED TO SAY:
I'LL GO WHEREVER YOU GO.

I SAID:
I HAVE TO CHECK WITH MY MOTHER.

I want to write on this one:
Since 2017, the European Union has invested 91 million euros in Libya, with the goal of reducing the influx of migrants coming from a country torn by endless civil war, where those fleeing are regularly subjected to arbitrary detention, torture, and slavery. How many deaths by drowning do our taxes finance?
I think you'll have to summarize that.

May I go to Lisbon on Saturday?

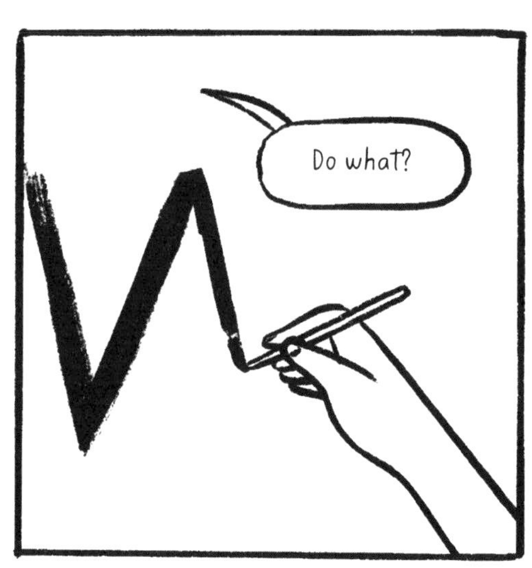
Do what?

To see an art exhibit with a friend from the theater.

And the demonstration?
What about it?

It's on Saturday! I need you there.
Why?

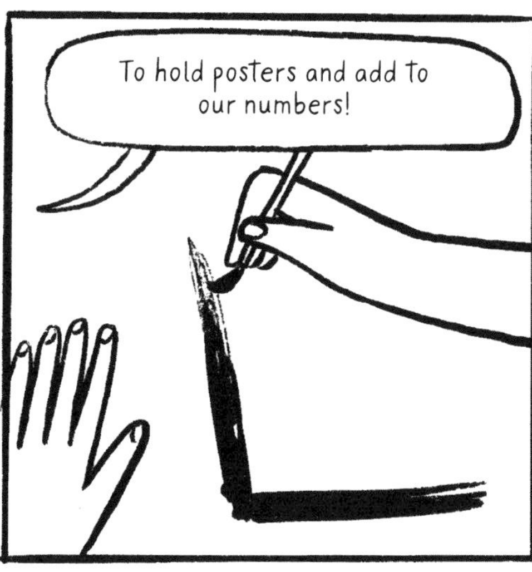
To hold posters and add to our numbers!

But I wasn't planning on going . . .

Why not?

I don't know. Too many people.
That's the point! What do you want? A private demonstration?

I don't want anything. You're the one organizing.

Fine, if you don't want to go, you don't have to help me.

But can I go to Lisbon?
Whatever you want.

Saturday morning we meet at the station. Still bleary-eyed, I bury my face in the hood of my rain jacket. Pardalita is ready to go, chattering away with our tickets in hand.

On the bus I try to find a comfortable position where my head doesn't bang against the glass. The radio plays music in English and condensation blurs the view from the windows.

Pardalita,

In a few months you're going away

in a bus like this one.

And things will
return to normal.

I won't always want to be near you,
because I won't be able to.

When we got off the bus
maybe it was that sense of
freedom
but everything outside seemed
so big.

The city buzzed, and
all the streets had
something to see.

Yellow trams snaked past us and then reappeared in miniature inside snow globes in a shop window. I asked myself when was the last time it actually snowed around a tram, because I can't imagine Lisbon as anything but sun and neon lights. I secured the jacket I'd brought, first around my waist, then on my arm, and finally tied to my backpack.

We passed a store that only sold hats, one that only sold gloves, and one that only sold cherry liquor. We saw a home appliance shop called Electric Moon and a Chinese restaurant called Paris.

I took advantage of stop lights to see who else was waiting. The city was filled with people who didn't look like anyone in my town. I passed streets jammed with cars, lit cigarettes on the ground, numbers written on tiles, and carpets of purple jacarandas.

(Fred once said the jacaranda is one of the few trees that has the same name in every language. Jacaranda is universal. No need to translate.)

The sidewalk, shiny and slippery, widened and narrowed as we traveled between staircases, avenues, and alleys.
The exhibit didn't open until late afternoon, so we had time to kill. We couldn't get lost because we weren't going far.

Wow

Do you think we can climb it?
There's only one way to find out.

This is kind of comfortable!

Do you have any music?
No, the battery's dead.

What would you like to hear?

Hmmm.

Antonio Variações seems fitting.

I only know that I am earth
raw earth ready to sow

On a wild and fallow hill

Mulberry fruit left to grow

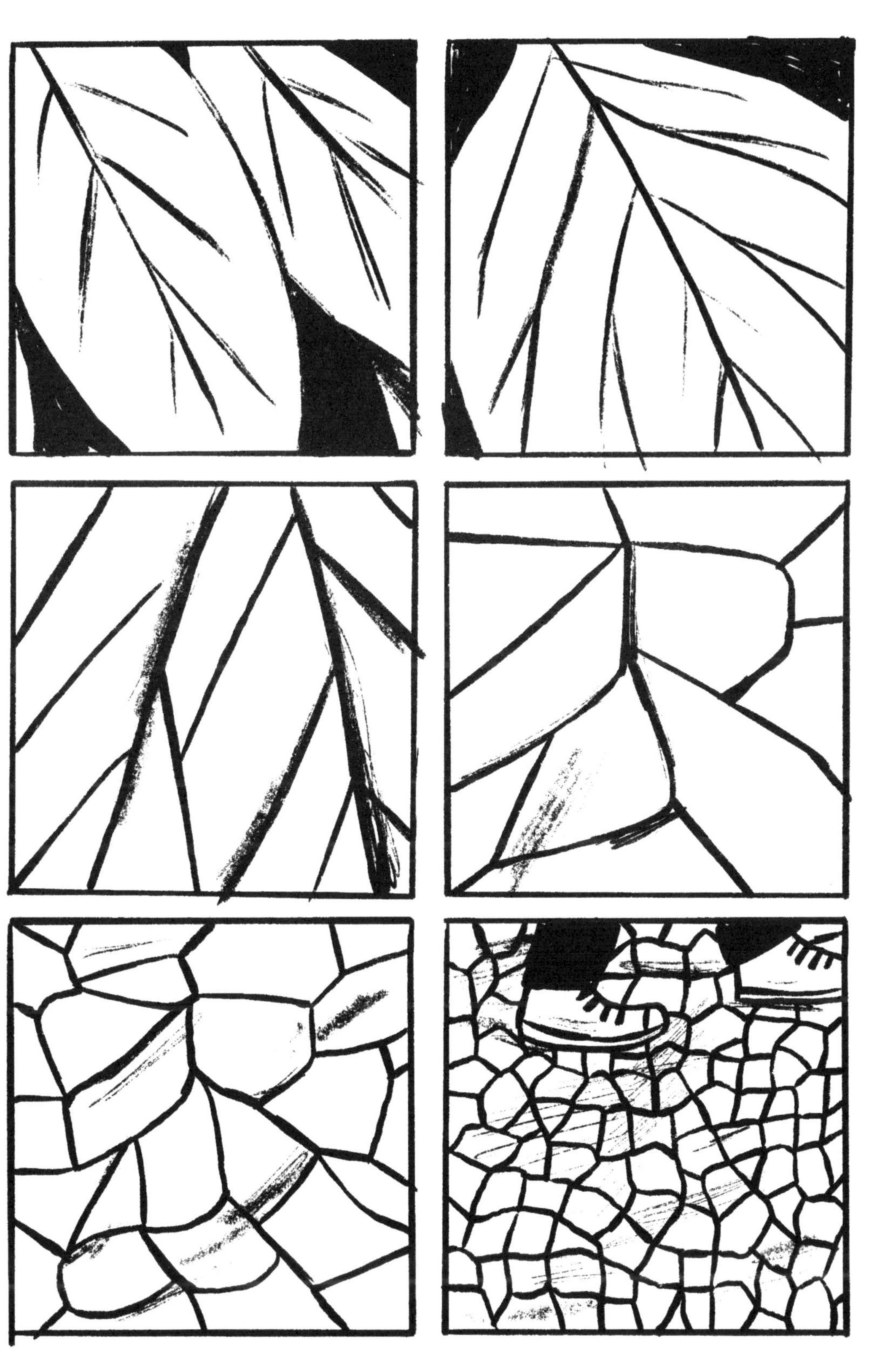

Are we going to the gallery?
We still have time. These things always start late.

I think we should see the river.
And the exhibit?
We'll go there next. You can't come here and not see the Tagus!

Pardalita, I don't comprehend you.

You're an irregular verb.
One to learn by heart.

GIVE

If you were on the other side, would you swim across?

p. 8 - The song from the TV commercial is "She's a Rainbow" by the Rolling Stones.

p. 158–159 - The painting that Pardalita is copying is "História Trágico-Maritima ou Nafrage" by Maria Helena Vieira da Silva.

p. 165 - The words that Raquel's mother chooses for her poster are from the article "Quantas mortes no Mediterráneo andamos a pagar?" written by Miguel Duarte for Fumaça.

p. 183–184 - The song that Raquel sings while in the tree is an interpretation of "Erva Daninha Alastrar" by Antonio Variações.

Joana Estrela

I am grateful to Rita. I began this book because of a story she told me, and I would not have finished it without all the support she gave me. To the people of the University of Porto Theater, who allowed me to watch their rehearsals. To Helena, who brought me to Lisbon. To Ana Pessoa, Mariana Pita, Mariana Pinhão, Sofia, Nicola, and Alex, who read sections of the book and encouraged me. To Joana Mosi, who read and reread the entire thing.

And to Nicolau, Valerio, and Mariana Malhão, who helped me find my ending.

Lyn Miller-Lachmann

Thank you to the folks at Levine Querido: Meghan Maria McCullough for bringing this project to me and to Nick Thomas for seeing it through; designer Jennifer Browne; and publicist Irene Vázquez and marketing director Antonio Gonzalez Cerna. And, of course, Arthur Levine, for his unfailing support of international literature in translation. However, none of this would be possible without the brilliant work of Joana Estrela and her publisher in Portugal, Planeta Tangerina.

Some Notes on This Book's Production

The art for the cover, case, and interiors was created by Joana Estrela using an iPad and Procreate. The type was set in Pardalita, a typeface created especially for this book by Estrela, along with selected instances of hand-lettering. The book was printed on FSC™-certified 120gsm UPM Fine woodfree paper and bound in China.

Production was supervised by Freesia Blizard
Book design by Joana Estrela and Jennifer Browne
Edited by Nick Thomas